Womble Winterland and other stories

The Ghost of Wimbledon Common

Orinoco the Magnificent

Womble Winterland

Adapted by Elisabeth Beresford

from the Wombles television series produced by CINAR and UFTP

Hodder Children's Books

a division of Hodder Headline plc

On Wimbledon Common, under the ground in their Burrow, live

The WOMBLES

The Ghost of Wimbledon Common

It was early one morning and Orinoco, Bungo and Tomsk were all getting ready to tidy up Wimbledon Common.

"Off you go, young Wombles," said Great Uncle Bulgaria, "but wait a moment, where's Wellington?"

"Sorry," said Wellington, hurrying out of the Burrow and tripping over in his excitement, "but I've just finished my new invention! It's a kind of washing-up machine. There's just one problem - there's a lot of soap bubbles coming out of it!"

Not far away, a newcomer to the Common was busy working on her tree-house. She hadn't met the other Wombles yet, and Bungo and Tomsk didn't know there was someone living in the tree above where they were tidying. The wind blew through the tree branches and Tomsk and Bungo looked up, wondering how a lot of junk had got stuck up there.

Then, suddenly, they heard something rustling behind them. They looked round and there it was . . . coming straight towards them.

"It's a ghost!" said Bungo. "Quick, run, it's after us!"

They ran as fast as they could to Great Uncle Bulgaria.
　　"It was white as a sheet!" shouted Tomsk.
　　"It chased me," said Bungo.
　　"What's all this about?" asked Great Uncle Bulgaria.
　　"A ghost!" said Bungo and Tomsk.
　　"Nonsense," said Great Uncle Bulgaria,
going back to reading his newspaper.

Bungo and Tomsk decided they would catch the ghost
to make Great Uncle Bulgaria believe them.
They asked Wellington to help by
building a Ghost Catching Machine.

"I suppose I could use the parts
from the washing-up machine . . ."
"Just hurry," said Bungo.

Tomsk and Bungo went off with a butterfly net and a fishing rod to hunt for the ghost. They didn't notice something white floating in the air behind them. When Bungo and Tomsk turned round and saw it they nearly jumped out of their fur. And at that moment the ghost fell on top of them.

There was a wild scramble and then Bungo managed to crawl out from underneath it.

"It isn't a ghost!" he said. "It's just an old sheet!"

Now while all this was
going on Wellington had
been making his Ghost
Catching Machine.
  "If any ghost comes
into our Burrow tonight
this will catch it!"
he said proudly.

That gave Bungo and Tomsk an idea. They put their heads together and decided to pretend to be ghosts that night.

So when everyone was asleep, they climbed out of bed and put their sheets over their heads.

"I'm a ghost," said Bungo, "whoooo!"

"I'm an even BIGGER ghost," said Tomsk, "WHOOOO!"

But no one woke up to see the ghosts.

So Bungo and Tomsk tiptoed through the Burrow until they reached the kitchen. And there on the table were some of Madame Cholet's special clover buns. They had to stop being ghosts for a moment just so they could eat one each. Delicious!

But at that moment Madame Cholet came into the kitchen.
"Ah ha!" she said, "two ghosts trying to steal my buns. Stop!"
And she chased the ghosts round the kitchen and then out into
the hall. And as they ran round the corner, Bungo and Tomsk
threw off their sheets. Tobermory heard the noise and came out of
his workshop. He held up the sheets.

"There are your ghosts, Madame Cholet," said Tobermory.
"Wait a moment, what's that noise I can hear?"

The noise was a banging on the Burrow door - in the middle of
a storm with lots of thunder and flashes of lightning. Tobermory
threw open the door and they all looked out nervously. There -
right in front of them – was a ghost!

Everybody was very startled for a moment and then the ghost threw off its cloak.

"Hello! My name's Alderney and I've just come to live in the tree house. I hope you'll let me shelter from the storm. OH! That's my sheet you've got there. It blew away this morning!"

"I'm very sorry, your ghostliness!" said Bungo and everybody started to laugh.

But that wasn't quite the end of the ghosts, because much later that night when everybody was tucked up in bed, Wellington's Ghost Catcher started to flash its light. Everybody woke up.

Bungo called out, "Madame Cholet, please come and turn off the machine! We don't want any more ghosts in our Burrow. Ever!"

Orinoco the Magnificent

One morning, a sleepy Orinoco was tidying up the Common.
There was a strange noise in the distance. But Orinoco didn't
notice anything until he almost tripped over an old box.
Inside was a magician's hat, a cape and a wand.

"It's a magic set!" said Orinoco. He put on
the hat, closed his eyes and waved the wand.
"Abracadabra!" he said. "Please
get rid of all this rubbish!"

And at that moment, a whirlwind
shot by with a 'whoosh', and dropped
all the rubbish into Orinoco's tidy bag.

Orinoco opened his eyes and
saw the full tidy bag.

"I'm magic!" he shouted. "I'm
Orinoco the Magnificent!"

Inside the Burrow, Tobermory had just had a message from the Wombles in the Thames Burrow.

"It says that they are sending us one of their young Wombles called Stepney. They want him to find out how much rubbish we clear up on the Common. It says that he's a 'Whizz Womble'!"

In the kitchen, Madame Cholet was busy making bramble cakes. Orinoco hurried in to tell her about his new magic powers.

"I can do magic now," said Orinoco. "I can make rubbish vanish . . ."

"Please vanish from my kitchen," said Madame Cholet. "I am very, very busy!"

"Yes, Madame Cholet," said Orinoco and he did vanish, with some of her cakes. He was just eating the last crumbs when Tomsk and Bungo came hurrying up.

"Guess what," said Bungo, "our tidy bags have magically filled themselves with rubbish!"

"My powers must be stronger than I thought!" exclaimed Orinoco. "It's me! I did it. I'm Orinoco the Magnificent!"

But nobody believed him. They just laughed.

The next day Alderney and Shansi were flying over the Common in the Womcopter. They were looking out for rubbish and really enjoying themselves.

"What's that?" said Alderney, looking down.

"It looks like a whirlwind!"

Far, far below them Stepney was whirling across the Common with his wheeliebarrow. This was his machine for picking up rubbish, and it was very fast indeed – fast enough to make a whirlwind when it passed by!

"I'm Stepney Womble. And I've come to show you how we tidy up in our Thames Burrow."

"If you think your Burrow is better than ours, let's have a competition to see who can collect the most rubbish!" said Alderney, who was really quite cross.

Of course, all the Wombles lined up
for the start of the race, with Orinoco
holding the stopwatch.
"One, two, three . . . GO!"

Away went Stepney with his wheeliebarrow and Alderney was just picking up an old umbrella when he whizzed past, taking the brolly with him, and she sat down with a thump.

Orinoco was waving his magic wand, but it didn't seem to be working because his tidy bag stayed empty. And at the end of the race, although the Wimbledon Wombles had worked very hard, Stepney had tidied up the most rubbish, so he'd won!

However, Wellington had just had one of his great ideas and off he went to the Workshop with Alderney. He was going to invent a tidying-up machine himself.

The machine was a skootboard and as soon as it was finished they
went to try it out.

The very next day Bungo, Tomsk and Orinoco were all lined up
ready to start work when they heard a strange noise, a sort of VROOM
VROOM, and straight towards them came Alderney and Wellington on
the skootboard.

"This'll show Stepney how fast *we* can work," said Alderney. "Please give me my tidy bag, Orinoco, and off we go. VROOM VROOM!"

Stepney had been working so hard that he thought he'd just have a little sleep before he got back to the Burrow, and he never heard Alderney come riding past.

Alderney scooped up all his rubbish and off she went. Stepney couldn't believe his eyes when he woke up and saw that his wheeliebarrow was empty. Very slowly he walked back to the Burrow.

"Never mind, young Womble," said Tobermory, "the others have just been playing a bit of a joke on you. Now then, let's start as friends all over again! Come in and have your supper."

Everybody laughed and clapped when Stepney walked into the kitchen and soon he began to laugh too. Especially when Orinoco said, "Now then - who wants to see *my* magic trick? It's called 'making your supper disappear!' VROOM VROOM!"

Womble Winterland

One morning when the young Wombles opened the door of the Burrow they got a big surprise. The Common had turned white overnight and it looked like a wonderful winterland.

"Snow!" shouted Tomsk, Bungo and Wellington and they began to throw snowballs at each other. Then Tomsk dived into the snow and pretended he was swimming.

But Orinoco didn't like it. "I think I'll go and help Madame
Cholet in the nice, warm kitchen."

　　But Tobermory said, "Tidying up work is outside, young
Orinoco. Off you go."

　　Tobermory turned to go back into the Burrow. 'Splosh!' -
he was hit by a snowball, thrown by Great Uncle Bulgaria!

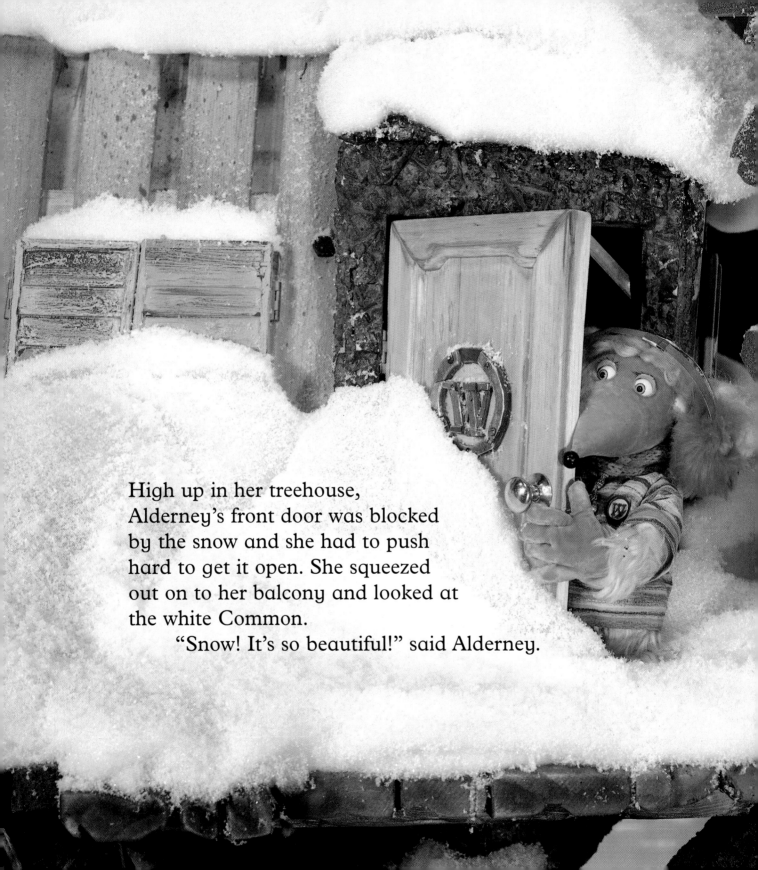

High up in her treehouse,
Alderney's front door was blocked
by the snow and she had to push
hard to get it open. She squeezed
out on to her balcony and looked at
the white Common.

"Snow! It's so beautiful!" said Alderney.

Alderney decided to go and see Shansi. But when she got down to the ground in her tree lift, she couldn't get out of the door. It was blocked by a big heap of snow.

"Help!" Alderney shouted, but nobody heard her.

Shansi was worried about her plants. They didn't seem to like the cold.

"I must move them indoors. I'll ask Alderney for help," Shansi said to herself as she set off for the treehouse.

Shansi plodded through the snow.

"Alderney, come and help me!" she called up to the treehouse.

"I need *your* help," Alderney shouted down. "I can't get out. My doorway is blocked."

"I'll go and get the others," said Shansi. "And I'll be faster if I turn your skootboard into a skiboard!"

The young Wombles had found hardly any rubbish.

"How can we fill our tidy bags when everything is covered by the snow?" grumbled Orinoco.

The others were trying harder than Orinoco and Tomsk found an old tray. He was sure it would come in useful!

While they were busy, Orinoco found a comfortable place for a nap, at the bottom of a bank.

"Look what I've found," shouted Bungo. "A copy of the Times, frozen inside some ice! Great Uncle Bulgaria will be pleased."

And he and Tomsk began to push and pull the block of ice down the bank.

Suddenly the ice block tipped over and sent Bungo
flying. The next moment he found himself sitting on top
of it as it slid down the bank.

"Oh, no! The tree!" called Tomsk.

And the ice block crashed right into it. Bungo was thrown into a pile of snow and more snow showered down on top of him. On the other side of the tree, snow fell on Orinoco until he looked like a Snow Womble.

The two snowy Wombles held each other up.

"Ooooh!" they moaned.

"Look! The ice block broke open and I've rescued the
Times for Great Uncle Bulgaria!" shouted Tomsk.

"Well, now you can come and rescue Alderney from
her treehouse," said Shansi, flying up on her skiboard.

"We've got to get there quickly in case it snows again," said Wellington. "I know, let's tie that tray to the skiboard and make it into a sledge!"

It was a bit of a tight fit, but they all squeezed on.

"Oh good, here they come at last," said Alderney.

The young Wombles used their sledge to clear the snow from her doorway and Alderney was free.

Next they rescued Shansi's plants, and then it was time to get back to the Burrow. Tobermory was waiting for them.

Tobermory hadn't forgotten that Great Uncle Bulgaria had thrown a snowball at him earlier, so now he decided to throw one back. But it missed Great Uncle Bulgaria and hit Bungo.

And in no time at all everybody was having a terrific snowball fight in their wonderful Womble winterland!

This collection first published 1999

Photographs and original artwork,
courtesy of FilmFair Ltd.
a subsidiary of CINAR Corporation

Copyright © 1997 Wombles Productions Inc.
(a subsidiary of CINAR Corporation) and HTV Ltd.
All rights reserved.
Text copyright
The Ghost of Wimbledon Common © 1998 Elisabeth Beresford
Orinoco the Magnificent © 1998 Elisabeth Beresford
Womble Winterland © 1999 Elisabeth Beresford

based on the scripts from the TV series.

The Wombles ® is a trademark of Elisabeth Beresford/FilmFair Ltd

is a registered trademark of CINAR Corporation

ISBN 0 340 75409 5

10 9 8 7 6 5 4 3 2 1

A catalogue record for this book
is available from the British Library.
The right of Elisabeth Beresford to be identified as the
author of this work has been asserted by her.

All rights reserved.

Printed in Hong Kong

Hodder Children's Books
a division of Hodder Headline plc
338 Euston Road, London NW1 3BH